COCO
The Adorable Puppy

Author:
Jacqueline Stavreski

Illustrator:
TullipStudio

Copyright:
© Jacqueline Stavreski 2020

All rights reserved. No parts of this book may be reproduced or used in any manner without written permission of the copyright owner except for the use of quotations in a book review.

To my daughters Angelique and Chelsea, never forget how amazing you are.
Love you to the stars and back.
Love Always Mum xoxoxo

Coco is an adorable puppy, she is charming and beautiful. She is white with black spots and she likes everything, especially her new family!

Angelique and Chelsea are both amazing at something. Coco wasn't. Coco had not found something that she was amazing at doing yet.

Chelsea is an amazing artist and creates magical masterpieces but Coco was only good at chewing on pencils and rubbers in her mouth and destroying them.

Angelique is amazing at baking the most delicious cupcakes, beautifully decorated with yummy icing. Coco was only good at licking any leftovers and scraps that fell on the floor. YUMMY!

The children are allowed to sit on the comfortable beanbags, lie down on their cool bouncy beds, sit at the dinner table, relax on the couch and Coco's favourite, go for a ride in the car! Coco frowned, she wasn't allowed to do any of those things.

She thought the reason she could not do any of those things was because she was not amazing at anything.. 'I'm not an amazing artist .....or amazing at baking cupcakes,' she sighed. 'I wish there was something I was amazing at!' If I was amazing at something maybe I could go for a ride in the car!'

Coco started to think of all the things she might be good at. After all she did try her best and help the girls! She thought about all the pencils and crayons she thought might be yummy to eat.; She knew she was good at chewing on the dozens of shoes that she had worked hard on to pull apart.

She also made an extra effort to gather up all the stuffed toys, chomping them into little bits and pieces and leaving them on all the floors in the house. Coco felt sad that she was not amazing at any of these things.

'Perhaps,' Coco thought... 'if I was amazing at some of these things , then maybe I could join the others and sit on the comfortable beanbags, lie on the cool bouncy beds, sit at the dinner table, relax on the couch and what Coco longed the most for, go for a ride in the car!'

She was determined to come up with just one thing she was amazing at but she could not. 'I wish I was amazing at something like Angelique and Chelsea,' Coco sighed.

Coco felt sad and that she was a disappointment to her family. Finally, after not being able to come up with anything at all, she decided to leave the house. Coco went to find her belongings, and she picked up her favourite bone and started digging her way out of the backyard. She felt so disappointed that she was not amazing at something.

All of a sudden, she heard a loud noise! It was someone crying inside the house. The girls were playing and had slipped over on to the wet floor. Coco swiftly ran inside to see both girls crying. Coco immediately started comforting them. She started kissing their faces and making sure they were ok, helping to push them up off the floor. Instantly, Angelique and Chelsea started to giggle and smile as Coco was kissing them excitedly. It made both of them feel better again!

You are such an amazing, loving puppy Coco, the girls cried out with joy. You always make sure we feel better when we are hurt and always protect us.

'Yes, I do always make sure you feel better when you are hurt and always protect you,' Coco thought. Coco wagged her tail finally, She thought to herself I have found something I am amazing at! Coco felt so thrilled and happy again. 'How silly of me to forget my own self-worth,' she smiled.

We love so many amazing things about you Coco, Angelique and Chelsea shouted out. You are our best friend!

Coco felt so happy and put her bone back in her special spot in the house and finally knew her family thought she already was amazing and loved her just the way she was.

Coco never doubted herself ever again. Coco was so excited when Angelique and Chelsea asked their Mum if Coco could ride in the car the next day. She felt the wind in her ears and fur and as she gave Chelsea a great big sloppy kiss, she realised .. everyone is AMAZING at something!
Coco was so excited to be able to go for car rides with her amazing family.

Coco realised she was AMAZING too.

Made in the USA
Middletown, DE
23 July 2022